The Boy who Lost his SMILE

Wendy Graham

To order additional copies of this book, contact:
Xlibris LLC
0800-056-3182
www.xlibrispublishing.co.uk
Orders@Xlibrispublishing.co.uk

Written by Wendy Graham

Illustrated by Julie McCrea

One morning John woke up feeling a little sad. He got dressed and went downstairs to his mum who was in the kitchen.

"Oh John, whatever is the matter?" his mum asked.

"Why?" replied John.

"You seem to have lost your smile" said his mum.

So John went outside feeling very miserable.

He shoved his hands into his
pockets, pushed out his bottom lip
and ran towards the duck pond.

Mrs Duck was sitting with all
of her baby ducklings.

She looked over and said "Quack. Quack.
What is the matter with you?"

John explained "I have lost my smile"

Mrs Duck said "Quack. Quack.
I do hope you find it."

John ran down past the gate and through the field where Henry the horse was grazing.

Henry neighed, so John stopped beside him.

"Hey, what's the matter with you?" asked Henry.

"Oh...I've lost my smile" replied John miserably.

John ran as fast as he could. He stopped by the river and sat down.

John began to cry.

A fish popped his head out of the river and asked

"What's the matter with you?"

John looked at the fish and noticed that his bottom lip was further out from his face than John's was!

John explained "I have lost my smile and I don't know how to find it."

Then John asked "What is the matter with you?"

The fish replied

"Nothing, I always look like this."

John rolled around laughing at the funny fish who remained quite sombre.

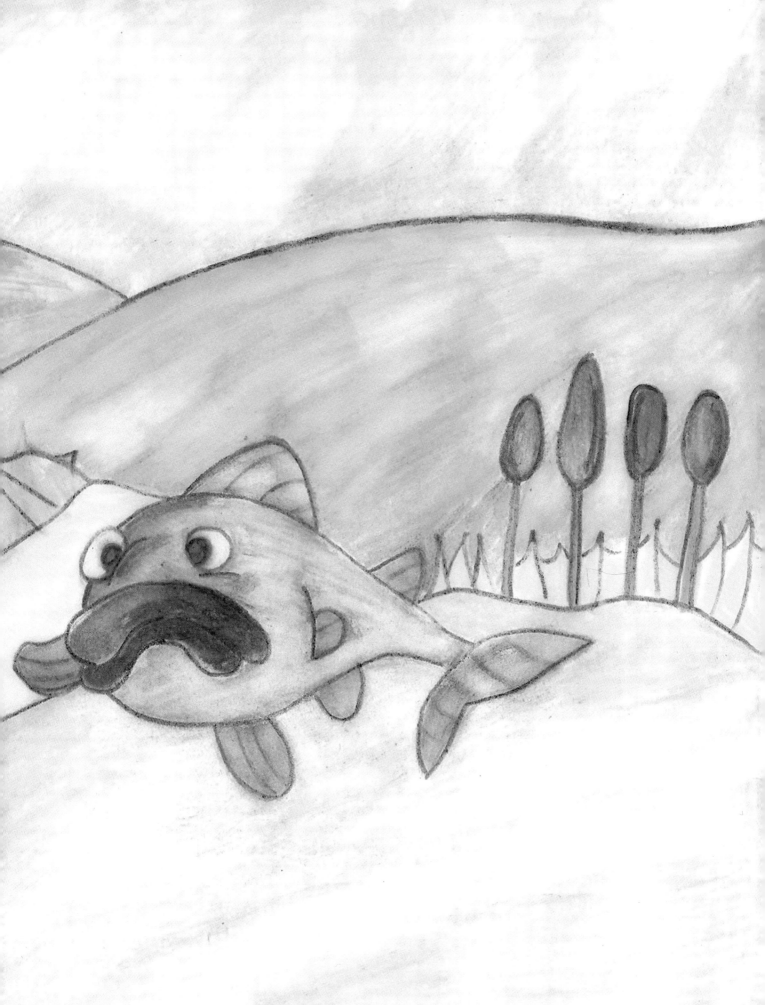

The fish said to John

"Look into the river."

John looked and saw his reflection. He saw
a beautiful beaming smile on his face.

He jumped up and shouted

"I've found my smile, I've found it!"

He ran home as fast as his little
legs could carry him.

He passed Henry and he shouted

"I've found my smile!"

Henry galloped after him
because he was so excited.

John ran through the ducks shouting

"I have found my smile!"

Mrs Duck was delighted and
quaked with excitement.

John ran into the kitchen and
threw his arms around his mum.

She took his little
face in her hands.

John said "I found it mum.
I found my smile. It was
really there all the time."

The fish represents Jesus.

The smile is the joy of the Lord

God bless you all.

Edwards Brothers Malloy
Thorofare, NJ USA
October 28, 2014